Mole's Moon

PUFFIN BOOKS
Published by the Penguin Group
Penguin Putnam Inc., 375 Hudson Street, New York, New York 10014, U.S.A.
Penguin Books Ltd, 27 Wrights Lane, London W8 5TZ, England
Penguin Books Australia Ltd, Ringwood, Victoria, Australia
Penguin Books Canada Ltd, 10 Alcorn Avenue, Toronto, Ontario, Canada M4V 3B2
Penguin Books (N.Z.) Ltd, 182-190 Wairau Road, Auckland 10, New Zealand

Penguin Books Ltd, Registered Offices: Harmondsworth, Middlesex, England

First published in Great Britain by Andersen Press Ltd., 1997
Published in Puffin Books, 1998

1 3 5 7 9 10 8 6 4 2

Text copyright © Hiawyn Oram, 1997
Illustrations copyright © Susan Varley, 1997
All rights reserved

Puffin Books ISBN 0-14-056416-0

Printed in Italy

Mole's Moon

Story by Hiawyn Oram
Pictures by Susan Varley

PUFFIN BOOKS

Littlest Mole was the littlest, and he saw what no one else saw.

When his brothers and sisters played in the dark tunnels around their house, they just saw dark tunnels.

When Littlest Mole looked out into the dark, he saw Glinting Things and Jaggedy Things and Things That Moved Around Mysteriously.

In the dark woods, he saw Long Gnarled Arms
and Long Graceful Fingers bending and waving
and dancing.

One night, in a dark stream, he saw the moon.
And when he tried to pick it up, it broke into a
thousand pieces.

Later that night, he jumped into his parents' bed and told them about all the things he saw.

"But little one," said his mother, "the dark is just *dark*. There's nothing much in it to see."

"And you certainly haven't seen the moon," said his father. "Everyone knows it lives in the sky, not in any stream."

"I saw one in the stream," insisted Littlest Mole. "I did."

"Then I think you'd better show us," said his mother. "Tomorrow night you can show us this moon of yours."

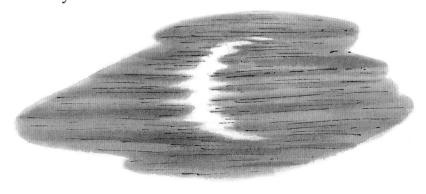

The next day, word got out. Littlest Mole was
taking his family to see a moon where a moon
couldn't possibly be.

Everyone wanted to go along —

Squirrel, Badger, Rat, Stoat, Fieldmouse, Frog,
Weasel, Rabbit, Hedgehog, and their little ones.
  By midnight, a crowd had gathered in the dark
woods beside the stream.

But as the night wore on and no moon appeared, they drifted off or fell asleep or complained to Littlest Mole's parents.

"He makes things up," grumbled Weasel.

"A downright fibber," grumbled Stoat.

"Or worse," grumbled Fieldmouse. "He sees what isn't there."

"He should have his eyes tested," said Rabbit. "Soon."

So the next day, Littlest Mole's mother took him to the Owl who did eye exams.

"Extraordinary," murmured the Owl as he tested. "It appears he can see in the dark."

"I told you," said Littlest Mole.

"But this is disastrous!" his mother wailed. "For us moles, the dark should just be dark. Velvety and dark. Seeing things in it can only mean trouble!"

"Then I have just the remedy," said the Owl, taking a blindfold from a drawer.

BLIMFF BUMP DIMMMPH was how Littlest
Mole got along with a blindfold over his eyes.

He walked into things.

He tripped over things.

He stumbled around things.

When he and his family joined Squirrel, Rabbit,
and Fieldmouse for a late-night picnic, he couldn't
see anything, especially not his moon.

So while no one was watching, he slipped away,
tore off his blindfold, and threw it into the stream.

And that's when he saw it.

Whiskers quivering in the bushes.

A snout behind the whiskers quivering in the bushes.

Beady eyes behind the snout behind the whiskers quivering in the bushes . . .

. . . all getting ready to pounce!

"LOOK!" he shouted as he ran back and tugged at his brothers.

"Oh, not your moon again," said one.

"Put your blindfold back on," said another.

"Look!" he cried to his mother and father.

"LOOK! LOOK! LOOK!" he tugged and pulled until at last somebody listened, somebody saw, and somebody yelled . . .

"FOX!"

"Well! Well! Well!" said Littlest Mole's father, when they were all safely home. "Maybe being able to see in the dark isn't such a bad thing after all! Though I must say, I still have my doubts about your moon."

"But why would I make it up?" said Littlest Mole.

"What do you say we try looking for it again?" asked his mother fondly.

And this time when everyone gathered to see Littlest Mole's moon, it did appear.

"Marvelous! Spectacular!" cried Squirrel.

"You must be so proud!" cried Rabbit.

"To have a Mole who sees so much!" cried Fieldmouse.

"Even a moon where a moon couldn't be," said Badger.

And while his parents enjoyed the praise, Littlest Mole spied something else. Very carefully, he picked it from the dark reeds and presented it to his brothers and sisters.

"My blindfold," he chuckled. "Just the thing for a game of Blind Mole's Bluff!"